own Tales

ERNEST ARI

This edition ©Ward Lock Limited 1989

First published in the United States
in 1990 by Gallery Books,
an imprint of W.H. Smith Publishers, Inc.,
112 Madison Avenue, New York 10016.

Gallery Books are available for bulk purchase for sales
promotions and premium use. For details write or telephone
the Manager of Special Sales, W.H. Smith Publishers, Inc.,
112 Madison Avenue, New York, New York 10016. (212) 532-6600.

ISBN 0-8317-0971-5

Printed and bound in Hungary

THE BRAMBLEDOWN TALES

BLACKBERRY
BUNNY

GALLERY BOOKS

An Imprint of W. H. Smith Publishers Inc
112 Madison Avenue

New York, New York 10016

You might hear the rabbits dancing

Chapter One

GONE OUT – BACK SOON

Far from the sea, but before you reach the mountains, lies the little village of Brambledown. Do you know it? On one side is a wood and on one side is a river. Over there is the road that brings visitors. And over here are the orchards where the bees hum when the blossom is on the trees.

Listen. When the wind comes whistling in your direction, you might be able to hear the sounds of Brambledown – the ringing of bicycle bells, the clank of milk churns, the striking of the village clock, the children in the school playground. You might even hear the birds singing, the moles digging, the mad March hare telling stories, the rabbits dancing . . . or you might hear Danger lurking in the wild wood.

Brambledown is full of animals. There are birds in the orchard, wild animals in the wild, wild wood, farm animals in the noisy farmyard and stables and cowsheds. There are cats and dogs curled in front of cottage fires. But one animal has the cosiest home of all. Blackberry Bunny lives indoors, with carpet to play on and windows to keep out the rain. Blackberry Bunny lives in Blackberry Cottage, in the second bedroom on the left. Of course he is a *toy* rabbit, with velvet ears and a cotton tail. But you would never know to look at him.

From his home, Blackberry can hear all kinds of outdoor noises. One day he said to himself, "I must go out and see the world for myself!" So he breathed on the mirror and wrote with his paw: *GONE OUT – BACK SOON.* Then he hopped downstairs and out through a window.

"I must see the world."

For the very first time Blackberry Bunny stepped out into the Big World. And wasn't it big! The ceiling was so high! And the walls were so very far apart!

Mr Blackbird flew by

"What a funny bunny!" cried Mr Blackbird as he flew by, way up high.

"Goodness!" said Blackberry. "How did you get up there? Don't fall, whatever you do!" Mr Blackbird only laughed and flew away.

Imagine if you had never been outdoors! Everything was so new and wonderful. The sun shone warmly on his velvet ears. The dew was cool against his cotton tail. "If the Big World is as wonderful as this, I don't think I'll ever go home!"

But just then a clock struck, a dog barked, a cock crowed and a door slammed. Blackberry was so startled that he ran for all he was worth.

He did not stop running until he was deep, deep in Brambledown Wood. The only sound was birdsong and a strange buzzing:

Buzz-buzz-buzz-zz-zzz.

"What an odd noise," thought Blackberry. He thought at first that a big red flower was trying to catch his attention, because the flower-head was nodding to and fro:

Buzz-buzz-buzz-zz-zzz.

He tried to peer into the flower with one eye and then the other and then with both. "Hello. Did you want something?" he said to the flower. And when it did not answer, he pushed his nose closer and shouted, *"Good morning, Flower! Were you buzzing at me?"*

"Buzz off! Buzz off!"

Suddenly Bonny Bee burst out of the flower in a panic. "Go away! Go away, you horrible great thing! Don't go poking in your nose where it's not wanted? Buzz off! Buzz off!"

A shower of pollen sprinkled Blackberry's nose and for the first time ever he sneezed.

Imagine – your first sneeze!

It was a very remarkable feeling.

"Bless you!" said a voice.

"Thank you. I thought my head had fallen off," said Blackberry. "What are you?"

"Well, *I'm* a rabbit, but – bless us! – what are you?" There sat a large brown rabbit – I mean a *real* rabbit – I mean Barney Brown and you know how big and real *he* is. "I'm Blackberry Bunny from the Second-Bedroom-On-The-Left, and I've come out to see the Big World. I've never been outdoors before today."

"So I see," said Barney Brown, "or you would never sit here, as bold as brass, in the middle of a clearing. Don't you know that the Big World is full of *Dangers*?"

Blackberry did not know why, but a shiver ran through his velvet fur that set his black ears trembling.

"Come and see this funny bunny!"

Chapter Two

NEW FACES

"What is a 'Danger'?" asked Blackberry, who had been nowhere and seen nothing before that day.

Barney Brown did not answer. He was far too busy looking Blackberry over. "Come and see this funny bunny!" he called softly. And at the edge of the clearing lots of little faces appeared.

"Seen it! Seen it!" peeped Mr Blackbird. "Saw it this morning!"

"How did it get so dirty?" asked Henry the Hedgehog.

"I'm not dirty! I'm made of black velvet," said Blackberry. "I thought all bunnies were black until I saw you. And I never knew rabbits could fly . . . Or are you a 'Danger' from the Big World?"

"I'm not a rabbit!" cried Mr Blackbird angrily. "And I'm certainly not a Danger. I'm a blackbird. Don't you know a blackbird when you see one?"

"Well, I'll know one next time," said Blackberry. "But I'm sure I never saw one in the Second-Bedroom-On-The-Left."

"I think our little indoors friend here is a very *unusual* bunny," said Barney Brown.

"I think he's very stupid," said Henry Hedgehog.

"What does stupid mean?" asked Blackberry, and Henry rocked so much with laughing that he rolled over and over on his spiny back and had to be rescued. "I never knew such a stupid rabbit before!"

"And I never knew such a *spiny* rabbit before," said Blackberry, ". . . or are you a 'Danger'?"

"Very *unusual*" said Barney

"I'm not a rabbit!" cried Henry hotly. "And I'm certainly not a Danger. Have you never seen a hedgehog before?"

"There aren't any in the Second-Bedroom-On-The-Left, I promise you. Not one. I would remember if there were," said Blackberry. And he was so friendly and so very interested

"Never seen a hedgehog?"

in Henry's spines that Henry forgave him at once.

"What do you eat?" asked the hedgehog.

"Eat?" said Blackberry Bunny who was, after all, a *toy* rabbit. He did not want to look foolish, so he said, "Ooo. This and that. What do *you* eat out here in the wild wood?"

"Sweet young grass," said Barney Brown nibbling the green shoots from between his paws. Blackberry nibbled, too. But although grass *looked* rather like a green carpet, it did not smell or taste like it. Not one bit.

"Worms, worms, worms!" cried Henry Hedgehog. "Yum yum!"

"Yuck, yuck," thought Blackberry, but he was far too polite to say it out loud.

"Me too! Me too!" whistled Mr Blackbird shrilly. "In fact I saw a nice juicy one as I flew down just now . . . And where do you think you are going, Mr Hedgehog?"

A moment later, Henry and the Blackbird were jostling and pushing each other in their rush to find a nice juicy worm. They were both very hungry!

They were too late. Maurice Mole got there before them.

Poor shy Maurice Mole was very startled when a big brown rabbit and a blackbird and a hedgehog and an odd black rabbit all arrived in a rush at the door of his burrow. It was too many people all at one time for a poor, shy mole to cope with.

Poor shy
Maurice Mole

He scuttled down his burrow and refused to come out.

"Where did that funny creature go?" asked Blackberry. "Was it a 'Danger'?"

Barney Brown laughed again. "That was Maurice Mole. He lives under the ground in a burrow – like rabbits do."

"I don't live in a burrow. I never heard of one before. Live underground? But it must be so dark and damp and dirty."

"Not at all! Not at all!" And Barney took Blackberry by his velvet paw and led him to his own burrow.

"It's awfully *dark*," said Blackberry. "Aren't you going to turn on the light?"

Barney Brown scratched his ear. Though he was clever as clever, he did not understand about turning on the light. "A burrow is a wonderful place," he said solemnly. "It's the only place a rabbit is safe from Danger." And in the darkness Blackberry's whiskers trembled at the sound of that word again.

Together the friends pulled him out

Chapter Three

THE QUEST BEGINS

No sooner did they climb out of the burrow than Blackberry spotted something: "Now I *do* know what that is!" he cried. "There's one in the Second-Bedroom-On-The-Left!" Away he went, and before Barney could stop him, he sprang over a row of reeds and
SPLASH!
into a pond of water.

"He's quite, quite mad," said Barney, scratching behind one ear.

"Oh help! Help!" cried Blackberry as he sank below the water a second time. "It wasn't a mirror at all!"

Henry Hedgehog and Mr Blackbird heard his shouts and came to see what had happened. Together the friends grabbed his paws and pulled him out.

They laid him in the sun to dry. I expect you know, that when a toy rabbit is wet he is a lot wetter than a real one.

"When *I* go out in the rain, one shake and I'm dry," said the puzzled Blackbird.

"I think he's quite mad," said Barney.

"Who's talking about me? Who's talking about me?" With a bound which shook the ground, Hoppity the Mad March Hare leaped along the bank. He held up his front paws like a boxer looking for a fight.

"Oh! Oh! It's a Danger and I'm too wet to run!" snuffled Blackberry Bunny.

A *Danger?*" cried Hoppity. "Hoppity-woppity! Never been so insulted in my life. A *Danger?!* What do you mean, you soggy little animal?"

So Barney Brown explained that it was Blackberry's first day out in the Big World. "He is a very stupi . . unsual bunny. He's never seen a pond before, or a hare or a burrow. And he doesn't know about Danger."

"Then it's time he learned," said Hoppity, with a mad sort of a grin. "This morning my very own sister, Hattie Hare met a great grinning, hungry, horrible *FOX*!"

"*EEEK*!" Everybody hid their eyes. Even Blackberry hid his, although he had no idea what a fox was.

"She was carrying a basket of *deliciousnesses* through the wood when – *GRRR!* – there stood the *fox*. She was terrified, of course. She dropped the basket and ran as fast as a hare can run – and everybody knows how fast *that* is.

Everybody nodded – even Blackberry, though he had no idea how fast a hare could run.

"Glad to say Hattie escaped."

"Phew!" said everybody.

"But out there now, in the deep, dark wood is her basket of *deliciousnesses*, and a great grinning, hungry, horrible *FOX*!"

Hattie Hare
escaped

"What's a basket?"

"What's a basket? What's a fox?" Blackberry wanted to know. "What's a fox? What's a basket?"

Hoppity Hare looked at him with big, round, brown, eyes: "You are right, Barney Brown. This here is a remarkably stupi . . . *unusual* bunny." Then he said, "Listen to me, oh small soggy one. Why don't you go and find my sister's lost basket? Baskets are wonderful. Baskets are full of things rabbits like to eat. But beware of the Fox! A fox is a thing that likes to eat rabbits — for breakfast, tea or dinner!"

"Let's all go! Let's all go looking for the lost basket!" cried Henry and Mr Blackbird.

But Barney whispered to the March Hare, "I know you, Hoppity. You made it all up."

"Hoppity-woppity. Maybe I did and maybe I didn't. Let's go and find out."

So all the friends set off to search for the basket Hattie Hare dropped when she was chased by the Fox.

"Didn't I say there was Danger in the wild wood?" said Barney Brown to Blackberry.

"Yes, but you didn't say anything about foxes," said Blackberry. "I understand now. A Fox is a Danger and a Danger eats you up. Aren't you afraid of being eaten?"

"Me? I'm not afraid of *anything*!"

"Nor am I!" cried Henry.

"Nor am I!" whistled Mr Blackbird.

"If I met a Fox, I'd stand up and fight," declared Hoppity Hare. "Hoppity-woppity!" and he biffed at the air with his two front paws.

It was a very hot day. Blackberry rushed this way and that, looking under bushes and into hollow trees. "Is it this? Is it that?" he asked, and the others replied:

"No, Blackberry. That's a mushroom," or

"No, Blackberry. That's a tortoise," or

"No, Blackberry. That's a bench-seat."

Soon everyone was worn out, and they all sat down under a tree to rest.

"I'll tell you a story," said Hoppity.

"Oh I know what *that* is," said Blackberry happily. "There were lots of *those* in the Second-Bedroom-On-The-Left."

"Shshshsh!" said the others.

"Once upon a time" (began Hoppity) "a fox caught a rabbit."

'I'm going to eat you up lickity-spit with a lick of the lip,' said the fox.

'Oh drat,' said the rabbit. 'I'm having such a bad day. To be caught by two foxes in one hour!'

'*Two* foxes?' said the fox.

'Yes. I was running away from the first one when you caught me. I think you may have to fight with the River Fox before you eat me up. He caught me first, after all.'

'We'll see about that! Where is this River Fox?'

'In the river, of course,' said the rabbit.

"I'll tell you a story," said Hoppity

"So the Fox went and peered over the river bank and what do you think he saw? . . . Another fox peering back up at him."

"It was his *reflection*, of course," whispered Henry in Blackberry's ear. "Like your 'mirror', ha-ha-ha!"

"Pay attention," said Hoppity sternly. "The fox growled at the River Fox, and of course the fox in the river growled back. The fox bared his teeth, and of course the River Fox bared his teeth, too. Woop! *Splash!* In went the fox to fight with the River Fox, and the water closed over his nose and his eyes and his ears. And away ran the rabbit, without a backward look."

"Bravo!" whistled Blackbird.

"Hurray!" shouted Henry.

"Three cheers for rabbits!" cheered Barney.

Blackberry clapped his paws and said it was a very fine story. And he picked some blackberries for Hoppity as a thank-you present.

"Why do they call you Black-berry Bunny?" asked Hoppity as he ate. "You don't look like a blackberry."

"I suppose it must be because my fur is so black and because I live at Blackberry Cottage. The brambles grow right up to the window at this time of year."

"You don't look like a blackberry"

Then the others thought it might be very enjoyable to live in a cottage in Brambledown Village, in the Second-Bedroom-On-The-Left.

But Blackberry could think of nothing better than to be out in the Big World on a quest to find a basket full of things to eat. He leapt up and began to search all over again. "Is it this? Is it this?"

"No, Blackberry. That's a deer."

"No, Blackberry. That's a bird's nest."

"No, Blackberry. That's Sam Squirrel."

Then Blackberry saw something small and green on the path. "Here it is, everybody!"

The 'basket' jumped away from him

Chapter Four

NO TREASURE?

"Here it is! Here it is! I've found the basket!" And Blackberry bent down to pick it up.

But the 'basket' jumped away from him: *HOP!*

He ran after it and tried again to pick it up: *HOP!*

"Oh do stand still, basket!" protested Blackberry.

"I'm not a basket!" croaked a wet, green voice. "I'm Oggie the Frog-og. How dare you call me a basket!"

The others laughed so much that Blackbird had to lean against Barney, and Barney had to lean against Hoppity, and Hoppity had to lean – ouch! – against Henry Hedgehog, who rolled himself up into a prickly ball.

"I'm awfully sorry," said Blackberry. "So long as you aren't a Fox or a Danger."

"I told you, I'm a frog-og. A frog-og! Frog-og-og! What a funny bunny you are!" And away hopped Oggie.

The search went on, and Blackberry kept thinking that he had found Hattie Hare's lost basket. But no.

"No, Blackberry. That's a boot."

"No, Blackberry. That's a kettle."

"No, Blackberry. That's a fence-post."

And each time, Blackberry ran away and hid. After a moment he would creep out of his hiding place, clutching his ears between worried paws. "Is it a Danger? Will it eat me up?"

"Dear oh dear, what a cowardly bunny," whistled Mr Blackbird.

"What a scaredy bunny," scoffed Henry Hedgehog.

"What a nervous bunny," said Barney Brown. "He's even scared straight out of his paws by an old boot!"

"He's scared of a kettle!"

"He's frightened of a fence-post ha-ha-ha!"

Blackberry made up his mind to be bold and brave and to find the lost basket before anyone else. But the more he went looking, the more he made mistakes: "I've found it! I've found it! Is this it?"

"No, Blackberry. That's a toadstool."

"No, Blackberry. That's a beehive."

"No, Blackberry. That's a raven."

"I know a story about a raven," said Hoppity Hare. "I know a story about a very stupid raven and a piece of cheese. Do you want to hear it? Hoppity-woppity! You're really going to enjoy this one!"

"Don't you believe one word he says!" said a voice high above their heads. The big black raven was perched on the branch of a tree.

"Hoppity-woppity!"

"That mad March Hare over there is a tale-teller! Don't believe his stories. There's not one word of truth in them!"

"Ah fooey!" said Hoppity sulkily.

"It's true," said Henry Hedgehog.

"I know," said Mr Blackbird.

"Everyone knows it," said Barney Brown. "But they're still good stories."

"Thank you, Barney," said Hoppity, cheering up.

Blackberry was very confused. "Do you mean you tell lies?"

"Indeed I don't!" cried Hoppity, throwing up his fists. "Hoppity-woppity! Call me a liar and I'll knock you down! I just tell stories to keep people amused."

But Blackberry's ears began to droop sadly. "You mean there *is* no basket full of deliciousnesses?"

Hoppity sniffed. "There *might* be. Somewhere. But I have to admit, I made it all up about Hattie Hare and the fox."

"He is *mad*, after all," called the Raven from the top of the tree. "All March hares are mad." And with a shrill cry – *CAW! CAW! CAW!* – she flew away.

"Don't believe a word!"

"Ah well," said Barney. "It was too hot for adventures anyway," and he flung himself down in the long grass, beside a stream. Mr Blackbird perched on a stone and had a long, cool drink. Henry Hedgehog curled up in a ball among some damp leaves and went to sleep. Hoppity Hare practised shadow-boxing against a tree. And Blackberry Bunny forgot all about the basket and Hattie Hare and the deadly dangerous Fox.

Little white clouds made funny shapes in the sky. One seemed to have four legs and a long bushy tail and pointed ears. "It reminds me of . . ."

But the cloud did not remind Blackberry Bunny of anything he could name, because he had never seen anything like it before. The outside world was all new to him.

"How beautiful the Big World is," he sighed, as a butterfly floated past his nose. "This is so much better than the Second-Bedroom-On-The-Left! I think I'm going to stay here for ever and never go home. I'm sure Barney Brown was making fun of me when he said there were Dangers waiting in the wild wood ready to eat me up. Dangers indeed! I haven't seen any Dangers. I've only seen a tortoise and a fence-post and a weasel and a boot and a mushroom and a toadstool and a bench and a bulrush and a bird's nest and a squirrel and a frog and a . . ."

"Who wants to race?" cried Hoppity Hare all of a sudden. He woke everybody up. "Can you race, oh small, silky, cotton-tailed Blackberry Bunny?"

"Just watch me!"

Everybody wanted to run races except for Henry Hedgehog. "My legs are rather short," he said. "If it's all the same to you, I shall be referee, I'll start you off and I'll decide who is the winner. Line up everyone! You must run once round that oak tree and the first person who gets back here to me is the winner. When I say 'Three', Go! On your marks! . . . One, Two, Three . . . *Go*!"

Off they went, as fast as they could go. Mr Blackbird swooped along between the ears of Hoppity Hare, Barney Brown rabbit and a very happy little toy rabbit made of black velvet.

Oh, it's such fun to run a race on a sunny day! The five friends hadn't a care in the world. The last thing on their minds that afternoon was the thought of Danger . . .

What very silly animals they were!

"How beautiful!"

There really *was* a fox...

Chapter Five

BEWARE! DANGER!

You see, there really *was* a fox in the woods that day – a big, ginger fox with a bushy tail and pointed ears and a great big appetite! He was waiting behind the big old oak tree, watching the rabbits and the hare and the blackbird and the hedgehog with beady, black eyes. He wore a wicked grin.

"Which shall it be?" he asked himself, licking his lips. "Will it be a bite of blackbird, or boiled bunny rabbit or sizzling hot hedge-hog? Or perhaps some tasty barbecued hare? Which will I catch? I hope it's that funny bunny with the shiny short black fur. I've never tasted anything like *that* before and it looks quite *delicious*."

Out he leapt from behind the big old oak tree.

Mr Blackbird saw the Fox and flew up into the tree.

Hoppity Hare saw the Fox and bolted into a bush.

Barney Brown saw the Fox and hurtled into a hole.

Even Henry Hedgehog saw the Fox and rolled himself up into a ball.

But Blackberry Bunny, racing for all he was worth, ran – *oof* – straight into the Fox. "Gracious goodness!" he said as he sat on the Fox's chest. "Look what I've found! I've tumbled right into a basket. I knew all along Hoppity's story was true."

"I beg your pardon?" said the Fox.

"No, no! I must beg yours," said Blackberry, "because I'm going to eat you all up." And he began to nibble the Fox's ear.

"Ow!" said the Fox, showing his teeth. "I think you have made a small mistake, mister rabbit. You see, I am a Fox, and *I'm* going to eat *you* up."

"Oh," said Blackberry with a gulp. "Are you a 'Danger', too?"

"Oh yes," replied the Fox with a grin. "I'm a very definite Danger to small rabbits."

Blackberry scratched one ear. "I thought you must be. You look so much like the Danger I met just now, swimming in the river. He promised to eat me up, too. That's why I was running away."

"What-what-what?" barked the Fox. "Another Fox? In my wood? Promising to eat my lunch? I won't stand for it!" Grabbing Blackberry by the ears, he strode to the stream. "Where's this foreign Fox? Show me!"

"There! There!" said Blackberry. "Lean over and you'll see him!"

So the Fox looked into the water, and he was so astonished by what he saw that he let go of his prisoner.

Away went Blackberry!

Away went Blackberry!

Behind him, as he ran, he heard the most gigantic *SPLASH*! The Fox had seen his own reflection in the water and jumped in on top of it, with a fearful roar.

It's lucky he could swim!

"You wait till I get out!" raged the Fox. He was furious. He spluttered and splashed and growled and howled. But it served him right, don't you think?

Blackberry's friends saw everything.

"How brave you were!" whistled Mr Blackbird, flying down out of the oak tree.

"Fancy remembering my story at a time like that!" exclaimed Hoppity Hare.

"How clever to make the Fox believe you!" cheered Barney Brown.

Only Henry Hedgehog uncurled from inside his prickles and said, "Uh? What happened? I wasn't looking. Somebody tell me what happened!"

They all agreed Blackberry was a very *unusual* bunny indeed.

When the Raven heard the news, she flew from end to end of Brambledown Wood and told all the other animals.

"What a magnificent bunny he is!" they all agreed. "And on his first day out in the Big World, too!"

Lucky he could swim!

Blackberry Bunny only looked down shyly at his paws and said, "Shall we finish our race?"

"My legs are trembling too much," said Barney Brown.

"My wings are weak with fright," said Mr Blackbird.

"My whiskers have gone all wobbly with the worry," said Hoppity Hare.

"Then I declare Blackberry Bunny the winner," said Henry Hedgehog. (Although to tell you the truth, Blackberry was shaking a bit too much to have run a race just then.)

The sun was going down. Purple evening shadows grew bigger behind them. The grass was wet with cold dewdrops. The little black velvet rabbit began to tremble.

He did not tremble because he was nervous or cowardly or afraid, of course. Oh no. He only trembled because he was getting a bit cold.

But the Big World *is* rather gloomy and dark after the sun goes down. And Brambledown Wood is full of a great many peculiar sounds. Listen!

crackle – hoot – scratch-scratch – howl!

"I think I'll go home to my burrow," said Hoppity Hare.

"I think I'll go home to mine too," said Henry Hedgehog.

"I think I'll fly home to my nest," said Mr Blackbird.

"Very wise," said Barney Brown the rabbit. "There are so many more *Dangers* lurking at night."

It was easy to imagine foxes and other Dangers looking out from between the dark trees, their beady eyes shining in the moonlight. "I think I might go home now too," said Blackberry Bunny.

"I might go home now"

So Barney Brown showed him the way back towards Brambledown Village, and Blackberry said goodbye to his friends, then ran all the way home.

Nobody saw such a small rabbit sprint along the village high street, because it was getting very dark.

Nobody saw such a dark-furred rabbit clamber up the blackberry brambles to the bedroom window of Blackberry Cottage and jump indoors.

Nobody saw him wipe away the words on the big bedroom mirror!

GONE OUT –
BACK SOON.

And nobody saw him snuggle under the covers of the big bed and fall asleep.

So nobody knew how a little toy rabbit once braved the Big World outdoors, with all its dreadful Dangers and deliciousnesses. Blackberry Bunny certainly did not tell anyone. He kept his visit a special secret.

But I know and you know that, now and then, Blackberry Bunny leaves the Second-Bedroom-On-The-Left in Blackberry Cottage, Brambledown, and goes back to visit his friends in Brambledown Wood.

He goes back, bold as brass, to smell the flowers and lie in the long grass when the sun is shining. But then I think you will agree with Barney Brown and Hoppity Hare and Henry Hedgehog and Mr Blackbird and the rest that he is a very *unusual* bunny!

A very unusual bunny

The Bram